A Firefly in a Fir Tree

to Max & Maude from Hilary 2003

for Lily & Steve
Kitty & Rich

HILARY KNIGHT

A Firefly in a Fir Tree

KATHERINE TEGEN BOOKS
An Imprint of HarperCollinsPublishers

On the first

day of Christmas

my true love gave to me...

a firefly in a fir tree.

On the second day of Christmas

DAY 2

my true love gave to me...

two silver pins
   and a firefly in a fir tree.

On the third day of Christmas

DAY 3

my true love gave to me...

Holiday housecleaning

three thistle dusters,
  two silver pins,
    and a firefly in a fir tree.

On the fourth day of Christmas

DAY
4

my true love gave to me...

four holly berries,
  three thistle dusters,
    two silver pins,
      and a firefly in a fir tree.

On the fifth day of Christmas

DAY 5

my true love gave to me...

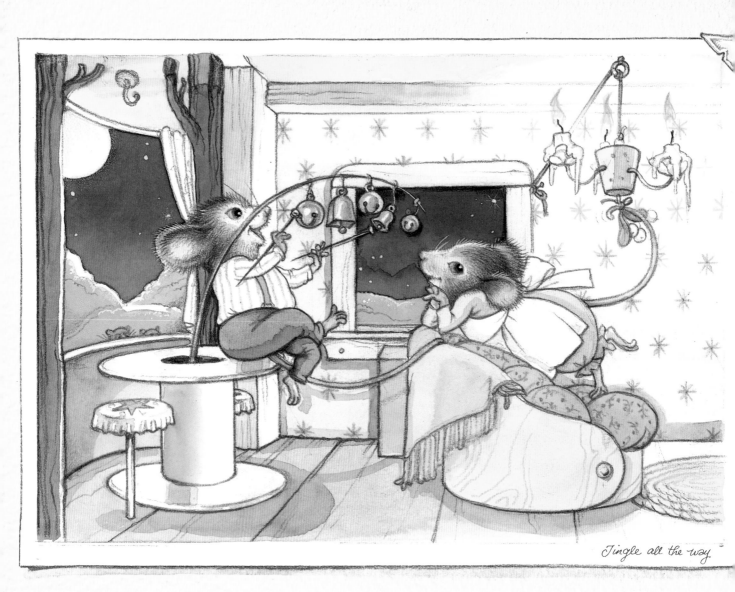

Jingle all the way

five golden bells,
   four holly berries,
      three thistle dusters,
         two silver pins,
            and a firefly in a fir tree.

On the sixth day of Christmas

DAY
6

my true love gave to me...

six wrens a-nesting,
  five golden bells,
    four holly berries,
      three thistle dusters,
        two silver pins,

and a firefly in a fir tree.

On the seventh day of Christmas

my true love gave to me...

seven spiders spinning,
six wrens a-nesting,
five golden bells,
four holly berries,
three thistle dusters,

two silver pins,
  and a firefly in a fir tree.

On the eighth day of Christmas

DAY 8

my true love gave to me...

eight crickets singing,
seven spiders spinning,
six wrens a-nesting,
five golden bells,
four holly berries,

three thistle dusters,
   two silver pins,
      and a firefly in a fir tree.

On the ninth day of Christmas

my true love gave to me...

Picnic on the Porch

nine nuts for nibbling,
eight crickets singing,
seven spiders spinning,
six wrens a-nesting,
five golden bells,

four holly berries,
   three thistle dusters,
      two silver pins,
         and a firefly in a fir tree.

On the tenth day of Christmas

my true love gave to me...

ten tree toads leaping,
nine nuts for nibbling,
eight crickets singing,
seven spiders spinning,
six wrens a-nesting,

five golden bells,
 four holly berries,
  three thistle dusters,
   two silver pins,
    and a firefly in a fir tree.

On the eleventh day of Christmas

my true love gave to me...

Winter workout

eleven feathers fanning,
ten tree toads leaping,
nine nuts for nibbling,
eight crickets singing,
seven spiders spinning,

six wrens a-nesting,
five golden bells,
four holly berries,
three thistle dusters,
two silver pins,
and a firefly in a fir tree.

On the twelfth day of Christmas

my true love gave to me...

Midnight musicale

twelve bees a-buzzing,
   eleven feathers fanning,
   ten tree toads leaping,
      nine nuts for nibbling,
         eight crickets singing,

seven spiders spinning,
six wrens a-nesting,
five golden bells,
four holly berries,
three thistle dusters,
two silver pins,
and a firefly in a fir tree.

Come with us and see...

... that
we had a
simply
wonderful
time.

A Firefly in a Fir Tree: A Carol for Mice
Text copyright © 1963, 1991 by Hilary Knight
Illustrations © 2004 by Hilary Knight
Printed in the U.S.A.

For information address HarperCollins Children's Books, a division of HarperCollins Publishers,
1350 Avenue of the Americas, New York, NY 10019.
www.harperchildrens.com
Library of Congress Cataloging-in-Publication data is available.
ISBN 0-06-000991-8 — ISBN 0-06-000992-6 (lib. bdg.)
Typography by Al and Drew
1 2 3 4 5 6 7 8 9 10
❖